Saturday Popular Concerts.

DIRECTOR—Mr. S. ARTHUR CHAPPELL.

Four Hundred and Ninety-third Concert.*

PROGRAMME FROM THE WORKS OF

Various Masters.

SATURDAY AFTERNOON, DECEMBER 5th, 1874.

Eighth Concert of the Seventeenth Season.

QUARTET, in A minor, Op. 43, for Pianoforte, Violin, Viola, and Violoncello.   *F. Kiel.*

(First performance at the Popular Concerts.)

Allegro moderato con spirito—A minor.
Adagio con moto—E major.
Scherzo, allegro con spirito—A minor; with
    Trio—F major.
Finale, vivace—A minor.

Mr. CHARLES HALLÉ, Madame NORMAN-NÉRUDA,
Mr. ZERBINI, and Signor PIATTI.

Allegro moderato (leading theme—A minor).

(Continuation of leading theme—strings only.)

The pianoforte accompaniment will speak for itself.

(Second theme—C major.)

Here Viola plays

(Tributary to second theme.)

Pianoforte in octaves.

In the development of the first part of the movement this tributary will again be recognised, in another form and in another key :—

(Tributary—pianoforte part only.)

The second part consists exclusively of an episode, the character of which may be indicated by a brief citation :—

Pianoforte.

Out of these materials the *allegro moderato con spirito* is built. The leading theme returns in the primary key, and the movement is conducted to a close in the ordinary manner.

Adagio con moto (leading theme—melody and bass only).

Pianoforte alone.

The stringed instruments now join the pianoforte in the theme. The composer then makes a transition into the key of G, in which an episode is introduced, of which the following condensed extract will give an idea :—

(Episode.)

The pianoforte has also an *arpeggio* accompaniment for the left hand, which does not need quoting. When the episode is developed, the leading theme appears again in E, now allotted to the viola, with a new pianoforte accompaniment; the episode reappears in C major, and a short *coda* brings the *adagio* to an end—of course in E, the primary key. No further examples are necessary.

Scherzo (theme).

(Episode—canon on the octave.)

There is also, further on, another episode, again in the

imitative style, with which the principal theme of the *scherzo* is worked simultaneously :—

(Imitation episode, No. 2.)

Pianoforte in octaves.

Viola. Theme of *scherzo*.

Theme.

Cello an octave lower.

The other instruments join in; but there is no space to cite more.

Trio (F major).

After the *trio*, the *scherzo* comes agin, as usual, without repeat.

Finale (leading theme—A minor).

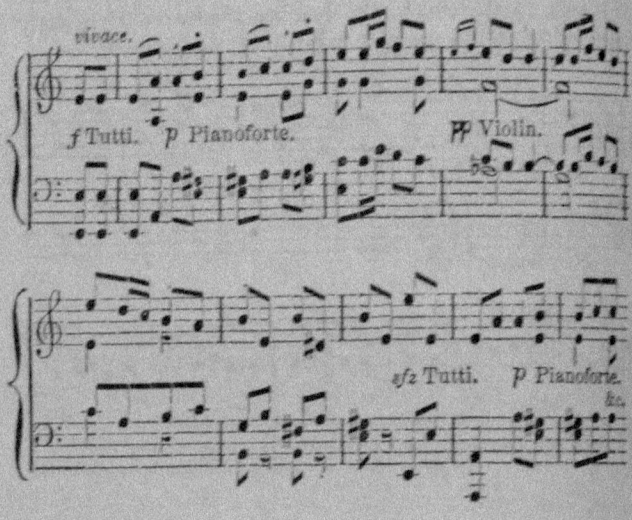

(Second theme—E minor.)

Violin and Viola.

The viola also has chords to fill up the harmony, while the violoncello plays the bass notes, "*pizzicato*;" but it is unnecessary to include either.

In the second part we have a new melody, treated in the fugal style, with which the leading theme is ingeniously mixed up (as in the example taken from the *scherzo*):—

More might be cited from this *finale*, but space is limited ; and quite enough has been given to enable attentive hearers to follow the whole with ease from beginning to end.

Herr Friedrich Kiel has written several important pieces of concerted chamber music, which, though very well known in Berlin and other parts of Germany, are just as little known in England and elsewhere. If he cannot be cited among the individually original composers, no impartial judge will deny the perfect freedom with which he handles his materials, a more convincing example of which could hardly be given than the quartet now introduced.

SONG, Madame OSBORNE WILLIAMS. *Proch.*

Clarionet Obbligato, Mr. LAZARUS.

"FLEECY CLOUDS."

The fleecy clouds on Heaven's domain,
They look at me, and then pass on
    To that sweet place where she alone remembers me;
In every sorrow, joy, or fear,
Oh, fleecy clouds! my prayer then hear—
    Oh, clouds! with you take me.

The little birds, with sweetest sound,
They fly along to that far land where her I found;
    Who gave me ever love's sweet song,
Received from me the ring so fair,
    And solemn vow to bind it true;
Then, little birds, oh! hear my prayer—
    Oh, birds! take me with you.

The rivulet glides gently by;
All tranquilly it hastens where my love doth lie
    When secretly she thinks of me;
And on the rivulet so clear,
    She daily looks confidingly.

Oh, rivulet! my prayer then hear—
    Oh, rivulet! take me!
The thoughts that never-tiring fly
    To that sweet place where dwells my love;
There joy beams on its gladsome race.

'Twas thus, with songs of love so rare,
    Her heart I gained so frank and free;
Oh, thoughts! my fervent prayer then hear—
    Oh, thoughts! with you take me!

SONATA, in E minor, Op. 90, for Pianoforte alone.*   *Beethoven.*

(Tenth performance at the Popular Concerts.)

Vivace e sempre con espressione—E minor.
Allegretto—E major.

Mr. CHARLES HALLÉ.

The Sonata in E minor, Op. 90, was dedicated to Count Moritz Lichnowski. Though one of the shortest, and consisting of two movements only, it is by no means one of the least beautiful of the series; and by those who divide the sum-total of Beethoven's artistic production into three styles, or periods, it is generally accounted the last pianoforte sonata belonging to the " Period No. 2."

Count Lichnowski, to whom the sonata in E minor is inscribed, was enamoured of an actress; and, if Schindler may be credited, Beethoven himself confessed that in composing it he had endeavoured to give musical expression to the history of this amour. The *allegro* was intended to contrast the passion which the Count experienced for the lady with the arguments that weighed against his desire to marry her; while the *allegretto* shadowed forth the happiness he eventually found in his union with the object of his affections. The first was to be called "*Kampf zwischen Kopf und Herz*" (" Contest between head and heart "); the second, "*Conversation mit der Geliebten*" (" Conversation with the beloved "). Count Lichnowski, on hearing the sonata, suspected that it meant something beyond abstract music—and, owning thus much to Beethoven, received the foregoing explanation. For the first time, Beethoven gives directions in his mother-tongue as to the manner in which he intends the movements of his sonata to be played. Over the *allegro* we read the following :—" *Mit Lebhaftigkeit und durchaus mit Empfindung und Ausdruck*" (which may be translated—" with vivacity, and throughout, with expression and sentiment"). The leading subject of this *allegro*, beginning as subjoined :—

* No. 27 of Beethoven's Sonatas, edited by Mr. CHARLES HALLÉ—Published by CHAPPELL and Co. 50, New Bond Street.

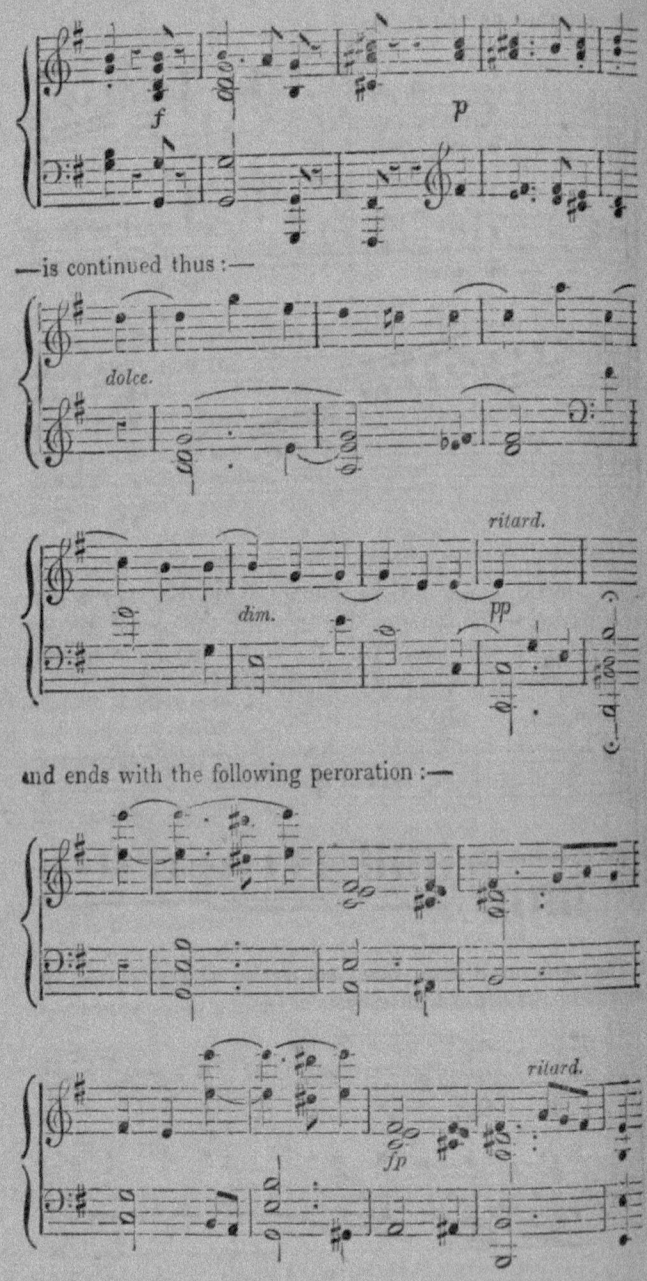

—is continued thus :—

and ends with the following peroration :—

We have then an episode :—

—the development of which leads to the prelude of the second subject—this time not in the dominant of the key, but in the key of B minor—the same as that in which the second subject is subsequently presented, viz., the minor dominant of the key of the leading theme and of the sonata :—

The theme itself is as passionate as the actress beloved by Count Lichnowski could have wished :—

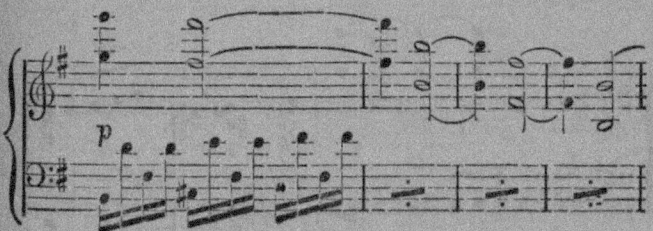

Further on, the continuation (if we may accept Schindler's anecdote for gospel) seems to portray the hesitation that distracted the mind of the amorous nobleman :—

The triad, G, B, coming thus unceremoniously upon the F sharp in the bass (bar 2), might well pass for the expression of a flat objection. The first part is not repeated. The second part commences with a new development of the leading theme, in the key of the opening, but passing almost directly to that of A minor, where, after a few bars, it is arrested as unceremoniously as the second subject (already quoted*) :—

Another flat objection—if anything beyond merely abstract music was intended by the composer. When this episode has been worked out, the continuation of the leading theme reappears, in a novel and enticing shape :—

After this is developed, a passage which, but for Schindler's story, might almost have been pronounced inharmonious, aided by such a clue, seems to convey with singular fidelity the indecision that prevented Count Lichnowski from at once grasping the happiness within his reach :—

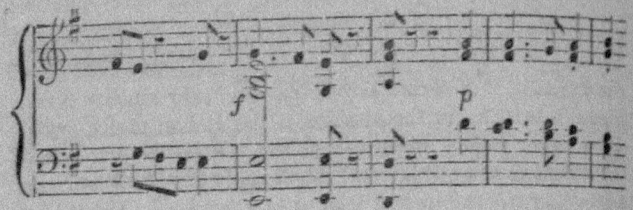

A passage in the first movement of *Les Adieux* is a sort of parallel to the foregoing—which essentially belongs to the third "style" or "period." Everthing now proceeds—allowing for the usual change of key (bringing back the second subject and its appendages in E minor instead of B minor)—as in the first part, until we arrive at the *coda*, in which once more we observe the portrayal of doubt and hesitation:—

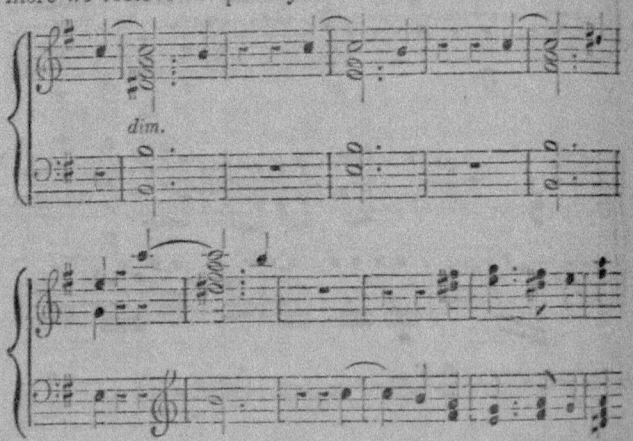

The movement then concludes with a repetition, *notatim*, of the peroration of the leading theme:—

The strife between head and heart disposed of, and heart having gained the victory, the rest of the sonata is "beautiful exceedingly "—serenely happy, indeed, as anything in music. The *allegretto* is to be played, according to the composer's precise direction, " *Nicht zu geschwind und sehr singbar vorzutragen*"—which, in the absence of the Italian prefix, would sound rather vague, inasmuch as the " *nicht zu geschwind*" (equivalent to *non troppo vivo*) might apply to *allegro* or *presto*, *andante*, or *adagio*, just as well as to *allegretto*. The " *Conversation with the Beloved*" assumes a most eloquent and engaging form. The leading theme is the essence of melody :—

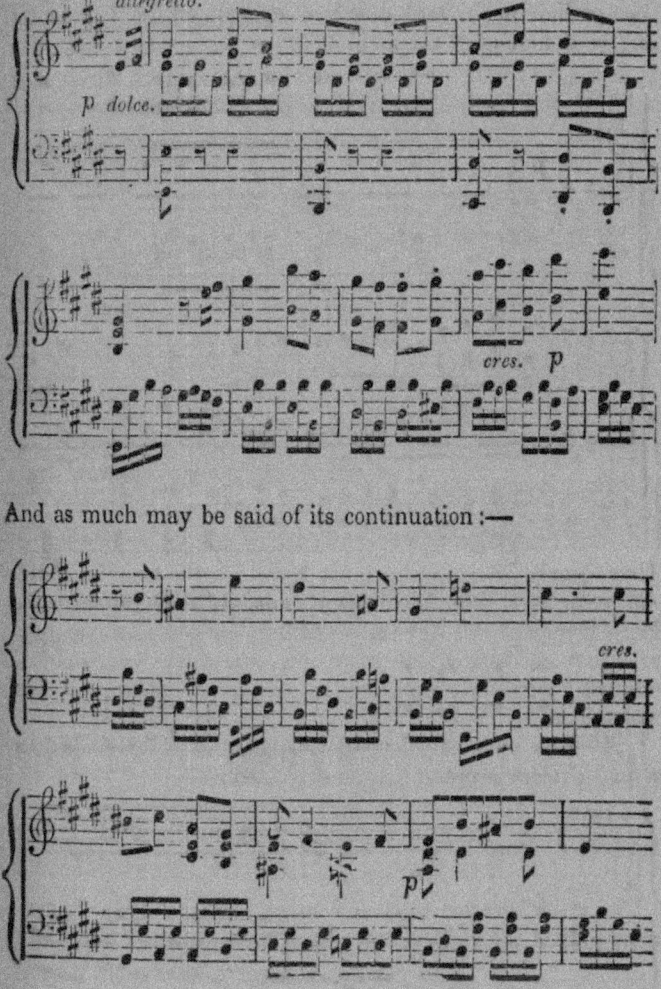

And as much may be said of its continuation :—

The passage to the dominant key is effected by means of an episode :—

The prelude to the second subject appears on the dominant of B (the dominant of the dominant) :—

How deeply Mendelssohn must have felt the beauties of this *allegretto* is shown by his own pianoforte sonata in the same key (E major). There can be little doubt but that the passage just cited, and still more emphatically its continuation, originally suggested the second *motivo* in Mendelssohn's first movement.

After an unusually long development of the prelude, the second subject is presented, as subjoined :—

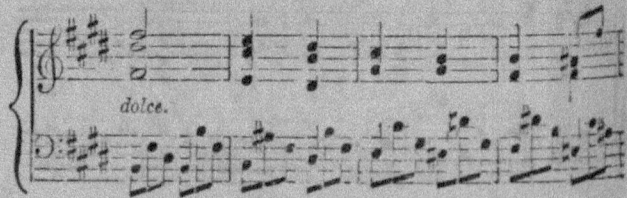

Concise as its preliminary is diffuse, this new subject, without a hint at elaboration, vanishes before the leading theme, the two sections of which are again repeated, with a full close in E. The second subject is then further developed in an episode, introduced by a bold transition from the key of E minor to that of C :—

The first four bars of the theme are here alternately presented in C major and C minor, and (through an enharmonic transition) in C sharp minor and C sharp major. Another episode (on the dominant of E) comes now :—

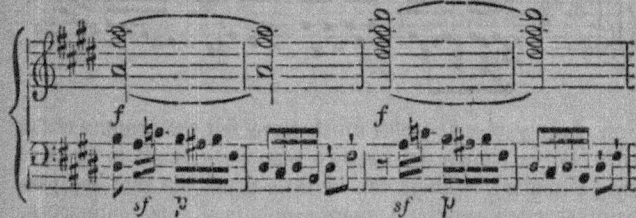

—and ultimately brings us once more back to the leading theme of the *allegretto*, both sections of which are given *in extenso*, as before. After this, the episode before quoted :—

—introduces a repetition of the Mendelssohnian second subject, and its prelude (in E instead of B).*   Further episodi-
cal matter, illustrating in the happiest way Beethoven's hatred
of tonic monotony, containing another enharmonic transition (*) :—

—and finally settling again on the dominant, with this graceful passage of strict double counterpoint :—

—leads to a fourth apparition of the leading theme, which—
thus transformed :—

* See Mendelssohn's pianoforte sonata in the same key (E major).

—is presented again without curtailment—the full close, however, being now indefinitely suspended :—

An episode, constructed on a dominant *pedale* (B) and formed out of the melody of the third bar of the theme :—

—still further suspends the cadence, which is at length attained, however, through the medium of the principal subject, the first section of which, freshly developed, brings the *allegretto* to an end, with the subjoined unaffectedly graceful passage :—

That Count Moritz Lichnowski should have loved and hesitated is of small moment to the world at large; but that his love and hesitation should have suggested this sonata, and enriched the art with a new masterpiece, is a matter on which Count Moritz Lichnowski may be felicitated; for though both he and the partner of his affections are long since dead, they live, and will live for ever, in the music of Beethoven.

The Sonata in E minor was composed in 1814, and advertised in the *Wiener Zeitung*, June 9, 1815 (by S. A. Steiner and Co.), as "*Beethoven-Sonate für P. F. Op.* 90." There is a copy in the handwriting of the Archduke Rodolphe, dated August 16, 1814; but this is not the date of the composition itself. It was first introduced by Mr. Charles Hallé, at the third concert of the fourth season—Dec. 2, 1861.

———

₊ Mr. CHARLES HALLÉ will perform on one of Messrs. JOHN BROADWOOD and SONS' Concert Grand Pianofortes.

———

SATURDAY POPULAR CONCERTS, ST. JAMES'S HALL.—On Saturday next, December 12, the Programme will include Beethoven's Quartet in A major, Op. 18, No. 5, for Strings; Schubert's Trio in B flat, Op. 99, for Pianoforte and Strings; and Beethoven's Sonata in G major, Op. 29, No. 1, for Pianoforte alone. Executants, Madame NORMAN-NÉRUDA, MM. CHARLES HALLÉ, L. RIES, ZERBINI, and PIATTI. Vocalist, Mr. SANTLEY. Conductor, Sir JULIUS BENEDICT. To commence at Three o'Clock.

Sofa Stalls, 5s. Balcony, 3s. Admission, 1s. Tickets and Programmes at CHAPPELL & Co.'s, 50, New Bond Street.

TWO STÜCKE IM VOLKSTON, in F and A minor, from
Op. 102, for Pianoforte and Violoncello.   *Schumann.*

(Third performance at the Popular Concerts.)

Mit Humor—A minor.
Langsam—F major.

Mr. CHARLES HALLÉ and Signor PIATTI.

These little pieces are Nos. 1 and 2 of *Fünf Stücke im
Volkston*, Op. 102.   They are as much in the popular tone
as Schumann could possibly make them, as will be seen by a
brief reference to the theme of each :—

No. 1.

281

(Episode.)

No. 2.

2 X

(Episode.)

The *Fünf Stücke im Volkston* are dedicated to Herr Andreas Grabau. As a motto to the first Schumann has put "*Vanitas Vanitatum.*"

The *Stücke im Volkston* were first introduced by Madame Schumann and Signor Piatti, at the nineteenth concert of the ninth season—March 2, 1867.

SONG, Madame OSBORNE WILLIAMS. *Schubert.*

"SCHLUMMERLIED." (CRADLE SONG.)

My darling child, whilst thou art sleeping,
  A mother's love shall watch o'er thee;
Close, then, thine eyes; cease thy sad weeping—
  Thy spirit soon at rest will be.

When thou art in mine arms reclining,
  My fond heart throbs with tender love;
Ah! when my years are fast declining,
  Wilt thou thy mother's comfort prove?

For thee, as yet, life hath no sorrows;
  But sunny days come to an end.
When thine, my child, bring cheerless morrows,
  Thou'lt come to me, life's dearest friend.

SEPTET, in E flat, Op. 20, for Violin, Viola, Clarionet, Horn, Bassoon, Violoncello, and Double Bass. *Beethoven.*

(By desire.)

(Twenty-seventh performance at the Popular Concerts.)

Adagio, leading to
Allegro con brio—E flat major.
Adagio cantabile—A flat major.
Minuetto; with Trio—E flat major.
Andante, Tema con Variazioni—B flat major.
Scherzo and Trio, allegro molto e vivace—E flat major.
Andante con moto, alla marcia, leading to
Presto—E flat major.

Madame NORMAN-NÈRUDA,
MM. ZERBINI, LAZARUS, PAQUIS,
WINTERBOTTOM, REYNOLDS, and PIATTI.

Of all the instrumental works of Beethoven, with the exception, perhaps, of one or two pianoforte sonatas, the Septet is the most familiar and the most generally popular in this country. Beethoven's affected depreciation of this magnificent piece in his later days will hardly lessen the enthusiasm of its admirers, when it is remembered that he himself made two new arrangements of the Septet—one as a trio for pianoforte, clarionet (or violin), and violoncello, another as a quintet for two violins, two violas, and violoncello. The original version (performed to-day) was dedicated to Maria Thérèse, wife of Francis I, of Austria. This Maria Thérèse must not be confounded with her more celebrated namesake, who died ten years before Beethoven was born.

The septet was first performed at a concert given by Beethoven (Vienna), on the 2nd of April, 1800, at which concert the symphony in C (No. 1) was also produced. It was published two years later by Hoffmeister and Kühnel (Leipsic), in two parts—the first part containing the first three movements, the second part all the rest.

The first *allegro* of the Septet is preceded by a short introduction (*adagio*), very much in the manner of Mozart, which, indeed, more or less prevails throughout the work.

The leading theme begins as follows :—

The second subject is in effective contrast :—

This spirited *allegro* is followed by a movement of a very different character—an *adagio*, melodious from first to last, and starting with the subjoined expressive phrase :—

This has a second subject of even greater melodic beauty :—

The *adagio* gives way to a minuet and trio, as unobtrusive as they are pretty. The theme of the *minuet* :—

—is well contrasted with that of the *trio:*

In No. 2 of the little pianoforte sonatas—Op. 49 (in G)—it will be found that Beethoven has, with some modifications, besides change of key, adopted the theme of the foregoing minuet for his finale:—

To the above succeeds a group of variations built upon the subjoined charming melody:—

287

The variations, five in number, are all in B flat major—
No. 4 excepted, which is in the minor. After these comes a
genuine *scherzo*, in the genuine Beethoven manner :—

This animated movement is wedded to a *trio* just as
sparkling and pretty :—

A brief introduction—*andante con moto alla marcia*, in
the minor key of E flat—then conducts to the *finale*, a *presto*
movement, the leading theme of which is as subjoined :—

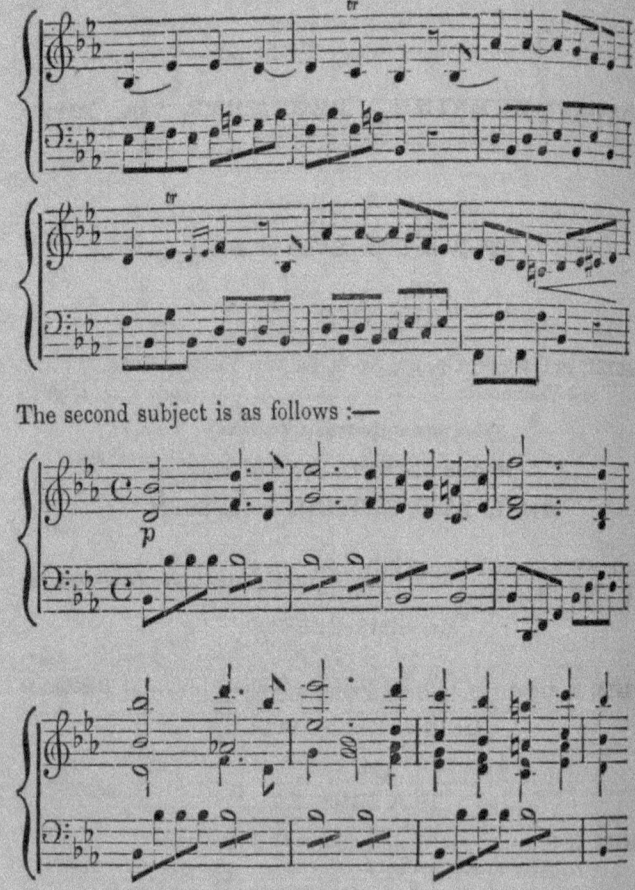

The second subject is as follows :—

The *finale* is quite as spirited as the first *allegro*, and a worthy climax to a work in all respects remarkable.

The Septet of Beethoven was first introduced by Herr Becker, Mr. Doyle, Mr. Lazarus, Mr. C. Harper, Mr. Chisholm, Mr. C. Severn, and Signor Piatti, at the fourteenth concert of the second season—March 5, 1860.

———

END OF THE FOUR HUNDRED AND NINETY-THIRD
CONCERT.

J. MALLETT, PRINTER, 59, WARDOUR STREET, SOHO. W.

MONDAY POPULAR CONCERTS.

MONDAY EVENING, DECEMBER 7th, 1874.

PROGRAMME.

PART I.

QUARTET, in C major, Op. 20, No. 2, for two Violins, Viola, and Violoncello .... *Haydn.*

(First time at the Popular Concerts.)

Madame NORMAN-NÉRUDA,

MM. L. RIES, ZERBINI, and PIATTI.

RECIT, " Deeper, and deeper still." } .... *Handel.*
AIR, " Waft her, angels." }

Mr. SIMS REEVES.

SONATA, in A flat, Op. 110, for Pianoforte alone .... *Beethoven.*

Mr. CHARLES HALLÉ.

PART II.

SONATA, in F major, for Violoncello, with Pianoforte Accompaniment.. *Marcello.*

Signor PIATTI.

SONG, " Ave Maria." .... *Schubert.*

Mr. SIMS REEVES.

TRIO, in F major, for Pianoforte, Violin, and Violoncello... *Gernsheim.*

(First time at the Popular Concerts.)

Mr. CHARLES HALLÉ, Madame NORMAN-NÉRUDA, and Signor PIATTI.

Conductor   -   Sir JULIUS BENEDICT.

www.ingramcontent.com/pod-product-compliance
Lightning Source LLC
Chambersburg PA
CBHW082053220626
47052CB00006B/1222